EAST *of the* SUN *and* WEST *of the* MOON

$\mathcal{E}$AST *of the* SUN *and* $\mathcal{W}$EST *of the* MOON

Retold by
KATHLEEN & MICHAEL HAGUE

Illustrated by
MICHAEL HAGUE

A VOYAGER/HBJ BOOK

HARCOURT BRACE JOVANOVICH, PUBLISHERS

SAN DIEGO   NEW YORK   LONDON

Library of Congress Cataloging-in-Publication Data
Hague, Kathleen. East of the Sun and West of the Moon. SUMMARY: A girl
travels east of the sun and west of the moon to free her beloved prince from a
magic spell. [1. Fairy tales.   2. Folklore—Norway]   I. Hague, Michael, joint
author.   II. Title.   PZ8.H125Eas   398.2′2′09481   80-13499
ISBN: 0-15-224703-3 (pbk.)
Printed and bound by South China Printing Company, Hong Kong
E F G H (pbk.)

For Meghan and Brittany,
our sun and moon

ONCE LONG AGO there lived a husband and his wife and their seven children. They had not enough to eat, and their clothes were patched and worn because they were very poor. The seven children were all quite beautiful despite their ragged clothing, but the loveliest of them all was the youngest daughter, who was as breath-taking as the first spring flowers.

Late one night in autumn, when the wild wind blew terribly against their little cottage, there came a tapping at their door. The family was huddled by the fireside keeping busy hand and mind and trying very hard not to hear the wind's horrible howl. Thus, it was a while before they heard the tap, tap, tapping on their door. The mother peeped out of the window but could see nothing because the night was heavy and black like the devil's heart and the stars were all in hiding. It was the father who went to the door and slowly opened it. On the doorstep stood a bear, the largest bear that the poor man had ever seen, and its color was purest white.

"Good evening to you," said the bear.

"Good evening," said the man.

"Would you like to be as rich as you are now poor?" asked the bear.

"Oh, yes," said the man eagerly, for he believed that a bear that could talk must be gifted with magical powers, and the granting of riches would surely not be beyond him.

"Then you must give me your youngest daughter," replied the bear.

The poor man was very troubled at hearing this. He wished to be rich and enjoy the finer life, but his heart ached to think of giving his lovely daughter to the strange white bear.

"I must ask my daughter," said the man, "for only if she consents will I do as you ask."

The man closed the door and told his wife and children about the white bear and the proposal he made. All of the children except the youngest became quite excited. They talked about the wonderful things that the great riches could buy, and they begged the youngest to accept the arrangement.

The mother and father also silently wished she would accept the white bear's offer.

"The white bear," they said, "must certainly be magic. And you will probably be made a grand queen somewhere. And, after all, your life must prove better with the bear than here, where we barely have enough to eat."

"No, no, no," repeated the youngest daughter, and she covered her ears so as not to hear their pleas.

The father went outside again and told the white bear to come again in a week to receive his answer. This the white bear agreed to do and then disappeared in the darkness.

All that week the family gave the youngest daughter no peace until she finally agreed to their request to go. When at last she made up her mind to go with the white bear, she put on a pleasing manner because she felt it was always best to accept things as they are and to do as well as one could in all situations. She washed and mended her clothes, which were rags, and made herself as smart as she could. Then she placed all she had in a bundle and awaited her fate.

Late that evening the white bear came. The youngest daughter was there to greet him.

"Do you come with me?" asked the white bear.

"I do," said the girl. She then seated herself on his back, and they left. They traveled the whole night in the direction of the distant mountains.

The sky was the rainbow colors of sunrise when the white bear finally spoke.

"Are you afraid?" he said.

"No, I am not," said the girl.

"Still, hold to me tightly," said the white bear, "for we have come to the very roots of the great mountains, and

The sky was the rainbow colors of sunrise
when the white bear finally spoke.

these parts are full of evil things. The black dwarves live here, as well as wicked trolls. But keep your courage because as long as you are with me, no evil will dare touch you."

They traveled on and on, and the woods became darker and darker. The trees had sinister looks, and there were strange rocks etched with runes. Every once in a while the girl thought that she saw yellow eyes blink at them from behind the great twisted roots of the trees.

At last they came to a great rock. The white bear told the girl that it was the heart of the wild mountains and inside was his castle. The girl climbed down from his back and watched as the white bear stood and knocked on the massive rock. While he knocked, he chanted in a strange language. Soon the girl heard a loud crack and watched in disbelief as the side of the mountain opened up. The girl followed the white bear inside the mountain and heard the opening close behind them. Inside many brilliantly lit rooms shone with gold and silver. They came to a large hall, which was so magnificent that words are not adequate to describe how splendid it was. The white bear handed the girl a silver bell.

"Ring this bell," he said, "and whatever it is you wish for will appear." Then the white bear left, and the girl was alone.

She'd had no food since leaving her parents' house and wished for something to eat. So she picked up the silver bell, and scarcely had the first chime sounded when a table appeared, set with the finest meal one could imagine. Never before had the girl tasted such food. After the meal the long journey she had taken with the white bear finally began to take its toll. She gave a long yawn and picked up the silver bell and wished for a comfortable bed. Again, no sooner had the bell rung than she was in a lovely bedchamber. There stood a bed ready made for her, which was as pretty as she found it was comfortable. It had pillows of satin, silk, and lace, and curtains of silk fringed with gold, and everything that was in the room was of the finest quality.

The room had but one window, which looked out upon the wild woods below and the blue mountains far away. It gave the girl a nice feeling to know that at least she could see the world that she had left behind. From her bed she gazed around at all of the fine things in the bedchamber, things only a princess could possess. Then she noticed a dark corner in her room. This corner was bare. It had none of the beautiful furnishings as did the rest of the room. Instead, there was only a stone slab upon the floor. In the morning she thought she would ask the white bear its meaning, but for now she wanted only to sleep.

She blew out the candle and pulled the soft blankets up to her chin. The moonlight drifted gently into the room through the window, and she was comfortably on the edge of sleep when she heard her bedroom door open. The white bear entered, walked past her bed and over to the stone slab in the corner. There was a twinkling of lights and the white bear disappeared, leaving in his place the dim form of a young man who laid himself down upon the stone slab and went to sleep.

This same occurrence happened every night when the candle's light was blown out. The young girl never spoke of it in the daylight, fearing that the white bear might become angry.

Except for this strange happening, all went well and happily for some time. But then the girl began to be very sad and sorrowful in her solitude, and she longed to see

This same occurrence happened every night . . .

her family again. The white bear asked the girl one day what it was that made her so sad and how he could make her happy again.

"As much as I enjoy your company," she said, "I miss my father and mother and brothers and sisters. I am very lonely because I cannot visit them."

"There might be a cure for that," said the white bear, "if you would but promise on your visit never to talk with your mother alone but only in the company of others. She will wish to speak with you alone, but you must by no means do so or you will bring great pain to us both."

The young girl gave her promise, and on the next day they journeyed back through the dark woods to her father's house. At last they came to a large mansion at the edge of the forest, and it was a pleasure to look at it.

"This is the dwelling of your family now," said the white bear, "but do not forget what I have said to you or you will do much harm both to yourself and to me."

"No, indeed," she said, "I shall never forget. I promise."

"Then I will come for you when one week has passed," the white bear said. And he left.

There were such rejoicings when she went in to her parents. All the family said that they could never be grateful enough for all she had done for them. Now they had everything that they wanted, and everything was as good as it could be. They all asked her how she was getting on where she was. All was well with her too, she said, and she had everything that she could want.

In the afternoon, after they had dined at midday, all happened just as the white bear had said. Her mother wanted to talk with her alone in her own chamber. But she remembered what the white bear had said and would on no account go. "What we have to say can be said at any time," she answered. But her mother at last persuaded her, and she was forced to tell the whole story of her life with the white bear as well. She told how every night, when the candle was put out, the white bear would enter her room and change into the form of a young man and how she never saw him because he always went away before it grew light in the morning. She added that she continually went about in sadness, thinking how happy she would be if she could but see him, and that all day long she had no companion except the bear.

The mother was dismayed at the girl's loneliness and fearful that the man who appeared each night was likely to be a terrible troll.

At last they came to a large mansion
at the edge of the forest . . .

"I will show you a way to see him," she said. "You shall have a bit of one of my candles, which you can keep hidden in your skirt. Look at him with its light when he is asleep, but take care not to let its tallow drop upon him."

All too suddenly the week was past and it was time to go back to the white bear's castle in the mountain. The young girl was sad to leave but was happy at having seen her family once again, all looking so very happy and well. She took the candle that her mother had given her and hid it in her skirt. When evening came near, the white bear came to fetch her. After they had gone some distance, the white bear asked her if everything had not happened just as he foretold, and she had to admit that it had.

"Then, if you have done what your mother wished," he said, "you have brought great sadness to both of us."

"No," she said, "I have not done anything at all."

The white bear said not another word as they journeyed through those dark woods on their way back to his castle in the mountain.

So when they had reached home and the young girl had gone to bed, it was just the same as it had been before. The white bear came into her bedchamber and shed his bear form in a twinkling of light, revealing again the form of the young man who laid himself upon the stone slab. Later, when she could hear his steady breath of sleep, she got up, lit her candle, and let its light shine upon his face. He was the handsomest man her eyes had ever beheld, and she loved him at once—so much that it seemed that she would die if she did not kiss him at that very moment. So she did kiss him; but while she was doing it, she let three drops of hot tallow fall upon his shirt, and he awoke.

"What have you done now?" he said. "You have brought misery on both of us. If you had but waited for the space of one year, I should have been free. I am a prince, but I have a stepmother who is a troll and who has bewitched me so that I am a white bear by day and a man by night. But now all is at an end between you and me, and I must leave you and go to her. She lives in a castle that lies east of the sun and west of the moon, and there too lives a princess with a nose that is three ells long. Now *she* is the one I must marry."

The girl wept and lamented, but all in vain, for he was bound to go. Then she asked if she could not go with him. No, he answered, that could not be.

"Can you tell me the way to the castle at least?" she asked. "And I will come to find you. That I may surely be allowed to do!"

"Yes, you may try. But," he said sadly, "there is no way thither. It lies east of the sun and west of the moon, and you would never find your way there."

When she awoke in the morning, both the prince and the castle they had lived in were gone. She found herself lying on a small green patch in the midst of the dark, thick woods. By her side lay the selfsame bundle of rags that she had brought with her from her own home. So when she had rubbed the sleep out of her eyes and wept till she was weary, she set out on her way. She walked for many and many a long day and night through the trolls' dark woods.

Finally she came in view of a very strange hut in the middle of the forest. The house seemed to grow out of a huge tree, and outside it an aged hag was sitting, playing with a golden apple.

The girl asked if she knew the way to the prince who lived with his stepmother in the castle that lay east of the sun and west of the moon and who was to marry a princess with a nose that was three ells long.

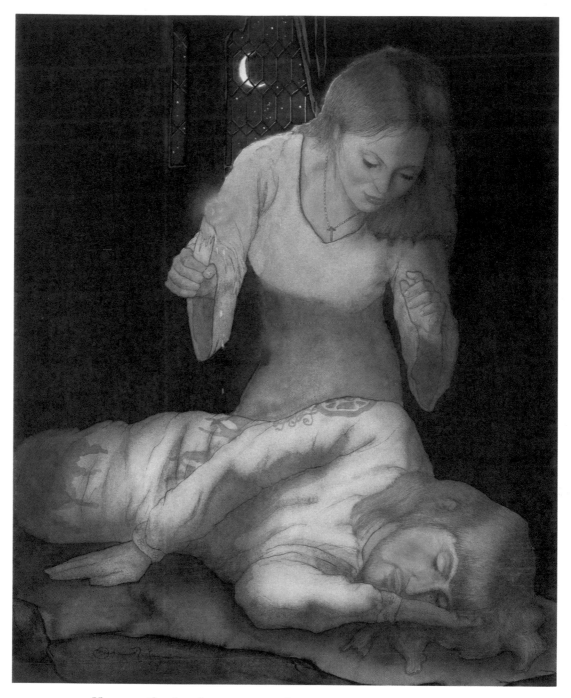

He was the handsomest man her eyes had ever beheld . . .

"How do you know about him?" inquired the old hag. "Is it you who ought to have had him?"

"Yes, indeed I should," she said.

"So it *is* you then," said the old hag. "I know nothing about him but that he dwells in a castle that is east of the sun and west of the moon. You will be a long time in getting to it, if ever you get to it at all. But you shall have the loan of my horse, and then you can ride on it to an old woman who is a neighbor of mine; perhaps she can tell you about him. When you have gotten there, just strike the horse beneath the left ear and bid it to go home again. Take this golden apple with you. You may need it. "

So the girl seated herself on the horse, and they rode for a long, long way until at last they came to a waterfall where another old hag was sitting atop a rune stone, combing her hair with a golden comb. The girl asked her if she knew the way to the castle that lay east of the sun and west of the moon; but she said what the first old woman had said.

"I know nothing about it, but that it is east of the sun and west of the moon and that you will be a long time in getting to it, if ever you get there at all. But you may have the loan of my broom, and it will fly you to an old woman who lives near me. Perhaps she may know where the castle is, and when you have gotten to her, just give the broom a kick and bid it go home again."

Then she gave the girl the gold comb, for she said it might be of use to her. So the girl seated herself on the broom, and it flew away over the woods to a great mountain. The broom came down in front of a cave where an old hag sat spinning yarn on a golden spinning wheel. Of this woman, too, she inquired if she knew the way to the prince and where to find the castle that lay east of the sun and west of the moon. But it was only the same thing once again.

"Maybe it was you who should have had the prince," said the old hag.

"Yes, indeed, I should have been the one," said the girl.

And, alas, this old crone knew the way no better than the others.

"But you may have the loan of my basket," she said, "and I think you had better ride to the East Wind and ask him. Perhaps he may know where the castle is and will blow you there. When you have gotten to him, just turn the basket over and it will come home again."

Then she gave the young girl the golden spinning wheel, saying that perhaps she would find that she had a use for it.

The girl climbed into the basket. It flew up into the sky, and it was a long and wearisome time before she arrived at the edge of a thick forest. There a great brown man stood as large as the tallest tree.

"Why have you come?" asked the East Wind.

The girl rose out of the basket.

"Can you tell me the way to the prince who dwells in the castle that is east of the sun and west of the moon?" she asked.

"Well," said the East Wind, "I have heard tell of the prince and of his castle, but I do not know the way to it, for I have never blown so far; but, if you like, I will go with you to my brother the West Wind. He may know the way, and he is much stronger than I am. Sit on my back, and then I can carry you there."

So she seated herself on his back, and they did go swiftly. Still, it took many days until they came to a great

. . . at last they came to a waterfall where another old hag was sitting atop a rune stone, combing her hair with a golden comb.

forest where they saw the West Wind standing. He was larger than his brother the East Wind.

The East Wind spoke and said that the girl whom he had brought was the one who ought to have had the prince at the castle that lay east of the sun and west of the moon. He said that now she was traveling about to find the prince again. So he had come there with her and would like to hear if the West Wind knew the whereabouts of the castle.

"No," said the West Wind. "So far as that have I never blown; but if you like, I will go with you to the South Wind, for he is much stronger than either of us, and he has roamed far and wide, and perhaps he can tell you what you want to know. You may seat yourself on my back, and then I will carry you to him."

So she did this and journeyed to the South Wind. They went a long, long way until they reached the edge of a large desert, where sat the South Wind. He was larger than either of the brothers, the East Wind and the West Wind. The West Wind asked him if he could tell the girl the way to the castle that lay east of the sun and west of the moon, for she was the one who ought to marry the prince who lived there.

"Oh, indeed!" said the South Wind. "Is that she? Well, I have wandered about a great deal in my time, and in all kinds of places, but I have never blown so far as that. If you like, however, I will go with you to our brother the North Wind; he is the oldest and strongest of all of us, and if he does not know where it is, no one in the world will be able to tell you. Sit upon my back, and I will carry you there."

So she seated herself on his back, and off he went from his desert domain in great haste, for they had a long, long way to travel. Finally they came to a land of ice, and they could feel the cold breath of the North Wind a long while before he came into view. The North Wind was by far the largest of the brothers—the East Wind, the West Wind, and the South Wind—and his hair and beard were wild and streaked with icy shades of blue.

"What do you want?" he roared.

And they froze as they heard him.

Said the South Wind, "It is I, brother, and this is she who should have had the prince who lives in the castle that lies east of the sun and west of the moon. And now she wishes to ask if you have ever been there and can tell her the way, for she would gladly find him again."

"Yes," said the North Wind, "I know where it is. I once blew an aspen leaf there, but I was so tired that for many days afterward I was not able to blow at all. But if you really are anxious to go there and are not afraid to go with me, I will take you on my back and try, if I can, to blow you there."

"There I must go," she said, "for if there is any way of getting there I must try, and I have no fear, no matter how fast you go."

"Very well, then," said the North Wind. "But you must sleep here tonight, for if we are to ever get there, we must have the day before us."

The North Wind woke her early the next morning and puffed himself up. He made himself so big and so strong that it was frightful to see him, and away they went, high up through the air, as if they would not stop until they had reached the very end of the world. Down below there was such a storm that it blew down woods and houses, and when they were above the sea, ships were wrecked by the hundreds. And thus they tore on and on, and a long time went by and then yet more time passed, and still they were above the sea. The North Wind grew tired, and more tired, and at last so utterly weary that he was

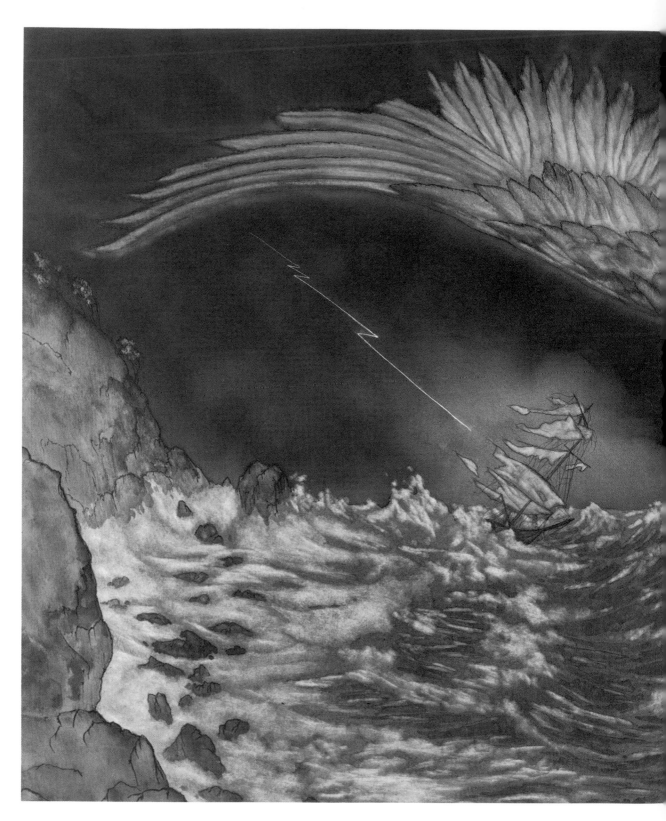

And thus they tore on and on . . .

scarcely able to blow any longer. He sank and sank, lower and lower, until at last he went so low that the crests of the waves dashed against the heels of the poor girl he was carrying. But they were not very far from land, and there was just enough strength left in the North Wind to enable him to throw her onto the shore, immediately under the windows of a castle that lay east of the sun and west of the moon. Now the North Wind was so weary and worn that he was forced to rest for several days before he could go to his home again.

The next morning the girl sat beneath the walls of the castle and played with the golden apple. The first person she saw was the maiden with the long nose, who was to have the prince. How ugly she was words cannot tell.

"How much do you want for that apple?" said the ugly maiden, opening the window.

"It cannot be bought for either gold or money," said the young girl.

"If it cannot be bought either for gold or money, what will buy it? You may say what you please," said the ugly princess.

"Well, if I may go to the prince who is here and be with him tonight, you shall have it," said the girl.

"You may do that," said the princess, for she had made up her mind to trick the girl.

So the princess got the golden apple, but when the girl went up to the prince's room that night, he was asleep because the princess had given him a sleeping drink. The poor girl called to him, and shook him, and she wept, but she could not wake him. In the morning, as soon as day dawned, in came the ugly princess with the long nose and drove her out again. That day she sat down once more beneath the windows of the castle and began to play with her golden comb. Then all happened as it had before. The princess asked her what she wanted for it, and she replied that it was not for sale, either for gold or money, but if she could go to the prince and be with him that night, the princess could have it. But when the girl went up to the prince's room he was again asleep, and let her call him or shake him or weep as she would, he still slept too deeply to wake. When daylight came, the princess with the long nose appeared and once more drove the girl away. That afternoon the girl seated herself under the castle windows and spun yarn at the golden spinning wheel, and the princess with the long nose wanted to have that also. So she opened the window and

*That afternoon the girl seated herself under the castle windows
and spun yarn at the golden spinning wheel . . .*

asked what she would take for it. The girl said what she had said on each of the former occasions—that it was not for sale, either for gold or money, but if she could get leave to go to the prince who lived there and be with him during the night, the princess could have it.

"Yes," said the princess again, "I will consent to that."

Now in the castle there were some good folk who had been carried off by trolls and imprisoned there. They had been sitting in the chamber next to that of the prince and had heard how a young woman had twice been there who had wept and called on him to no avail, and they told the prince of this. So that evening, when the princess came once more with her sleeping drink, he pretended to drink, but threw it away behind him, for now he suspected why she had brought it. So when the girl came into the prince's room, this time he was awake, and she was able to tell him how she had come there.

"You have come just in time!" said the prince. "Tomorrow I am to be married to the ugly princess, and you alone can save me. Now listen carefully to my plan. I will say to my stepmother that before I marry, I want to see what my bride can do. I will ask her then to wash the shirt that has the three drops of tallow on it. This she will consent to do, for she does not know that it is you who let the tallow fall on it or that no one can wash it out but one born of good folk. It cannot be done by one of a pack of trolls. Then I will say that no one shall ever be my bride but the woman who can do this, and I know that *you* can."

There was great joy and gladness between them all that night as they talked of the wonderful life that they would share when they were married.

The next day, when the wedding was to take place, the prince said as planned, "I must see what my bride can do."

"That you may do," said the stepmother, who was a troll hag and even uglier than the princess with the nose three ells long.

"I have a fine shirt that I want to wear as my wedding shirt, but three drops of tallow have somehow gotten upon it and must be washed away. I have vowed that I will marry no one but the woman who is able to do it," said the prince, "for if she cannot do that, she is not worth having."

"Well, that is a very small matter," said the stepmother, and the ugly princess agreed to do it. She immediately began to wash the shirt, but the more she washed and rubbed, the larger grew the spots.

"Ah! You cannot wash at all!" said the old troll hag. "Give it to me."

But she too had not had the shirt very long in her hands before it looked worse still, and the more she washed it and rubbed it, the larger and blacker grew the spots.

So the other trolls tried as well to wash it, and what a frenzy they made trying to clean the shirt. But the more they tried, the blacker and uglier it grew, until at length it was as black as if it had been up the chimney.

"Oh," cried the prince, "not one of you is good for anything at all! There is a beggar girl sitting outside the window, and I will be bound that she can wash better than any of you. Come in. You, girl, there!" he cried.

So she came in.

"Can you wash this shirt clean?" he asked.

"Oh, I do not know," she said, "but I will try." And no sooner had she taken the shirt and dipped it in the water than it was white as driven snow, and even whiter than that.

"It is you who shall be my princess!" said the prince.

. . . and what a frenzy they made trying to clean the shirt.

Then the old troll hag flew into such a rage that she burst, and the princess with the long nose and all the little trolls must have burst too, for they have never been heard of since.

The prince and his new bride set free all the good folk who were imprisoned there, and then a rainbow appeared and carried them, and all the gold and silver they could hold, far away from the castle that lay east of the sun and west of the moon.

MICHAEL HAGUE, author and illustrator, was born in Los Angeles and attended the Art Center College of Design in Pasadena, from which he graduated with honors. Among the books he has illustrated for HBJ are *Demetrius and the Golden Goblet*, *The Man Who Kept House*, *The Legend of the Veery Bird*, and Carl Sandburg's *Rootabaga Stories*.

KATHLEEN HAGUE, coauthor, was born in Ventura, California, and also attended the Art Center College of Design. She is an artist and photographer.

The Hagues live with their three children, Meghan, Brittany, and Devon, in Colorado Springs, Colorado.